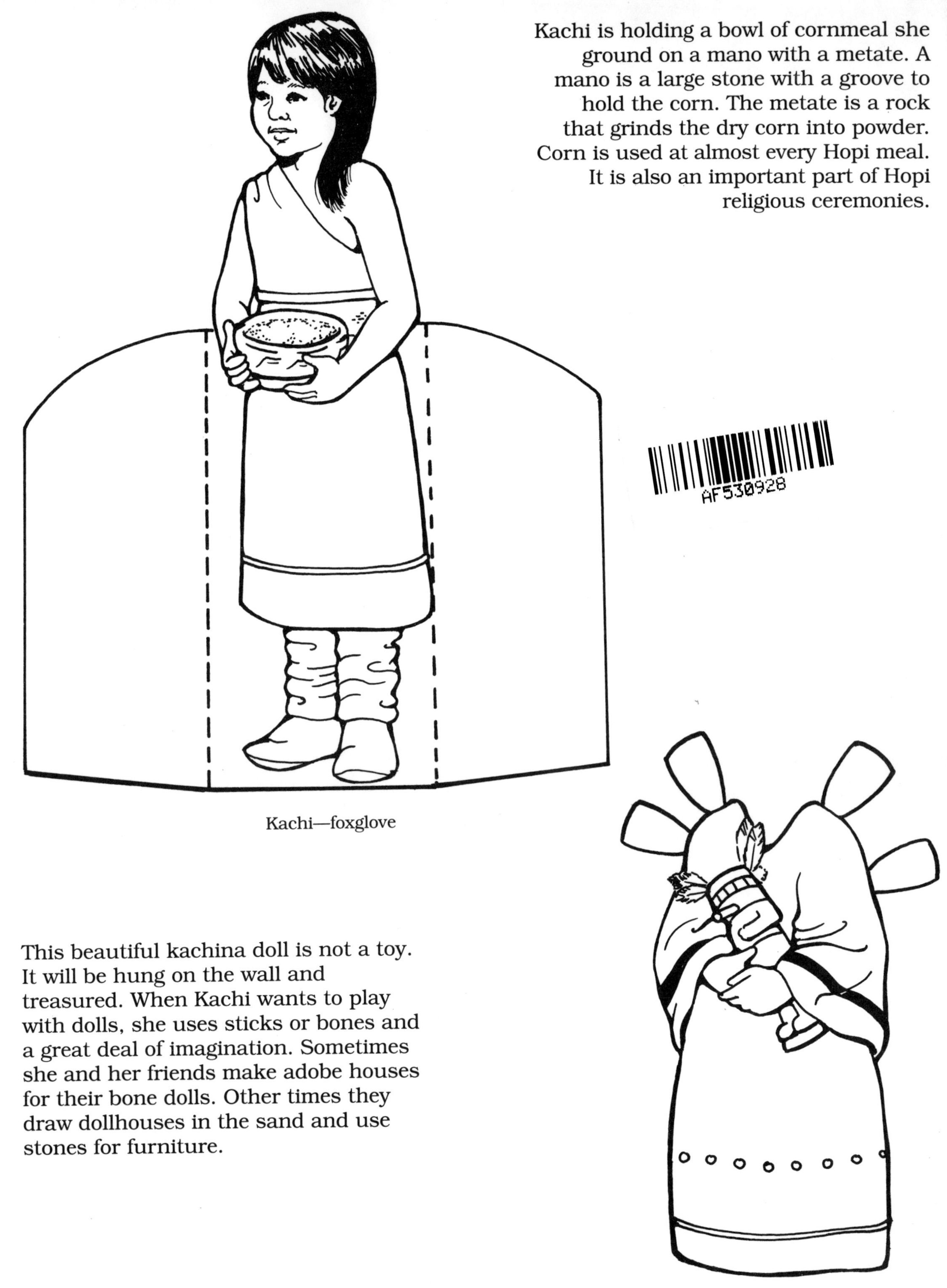

Kachi is holding a bowl of cornmeal she ground on a mano with a metate. A mano is a large stone with a groove to hold the corn. The metate is a rock that grinds the dry corn into powder. Corn is used at almost every Hopi meal. It is also an important part of Hopi religious ceremonies.

Kachi—foxglove

This beautiful kachina doll is not a toy. It will be hung on the wall and treasured. When Kachi wants to play with dolls, she uses sticks or bones and a great deal of imagination. Sometimes she and her friends make adobe houses for their bone dolls. Other times they draw dollhouses in the sand and use stones for furniture.

It is Kachi's job to watch over her brother, Tawakchi and her sister, Cuya. Kachi takes the children out to play and makes sure they stay away from fire or from the steep sides of the mesa. When Cuya or Tawakchi is tired Kachi carries them on her back.

Tawakchi—sweet corn

Kachi is going to dance in the butterfly dance! She is dressed in her prettiest dress and jewelry. On her head she wears a beautiful tablita that her uncle painted. For many weeks she and her friends practiced the butterfly dance in the kiva. Now they will dance and sing all day long. They will stop and feast at each house in the village.

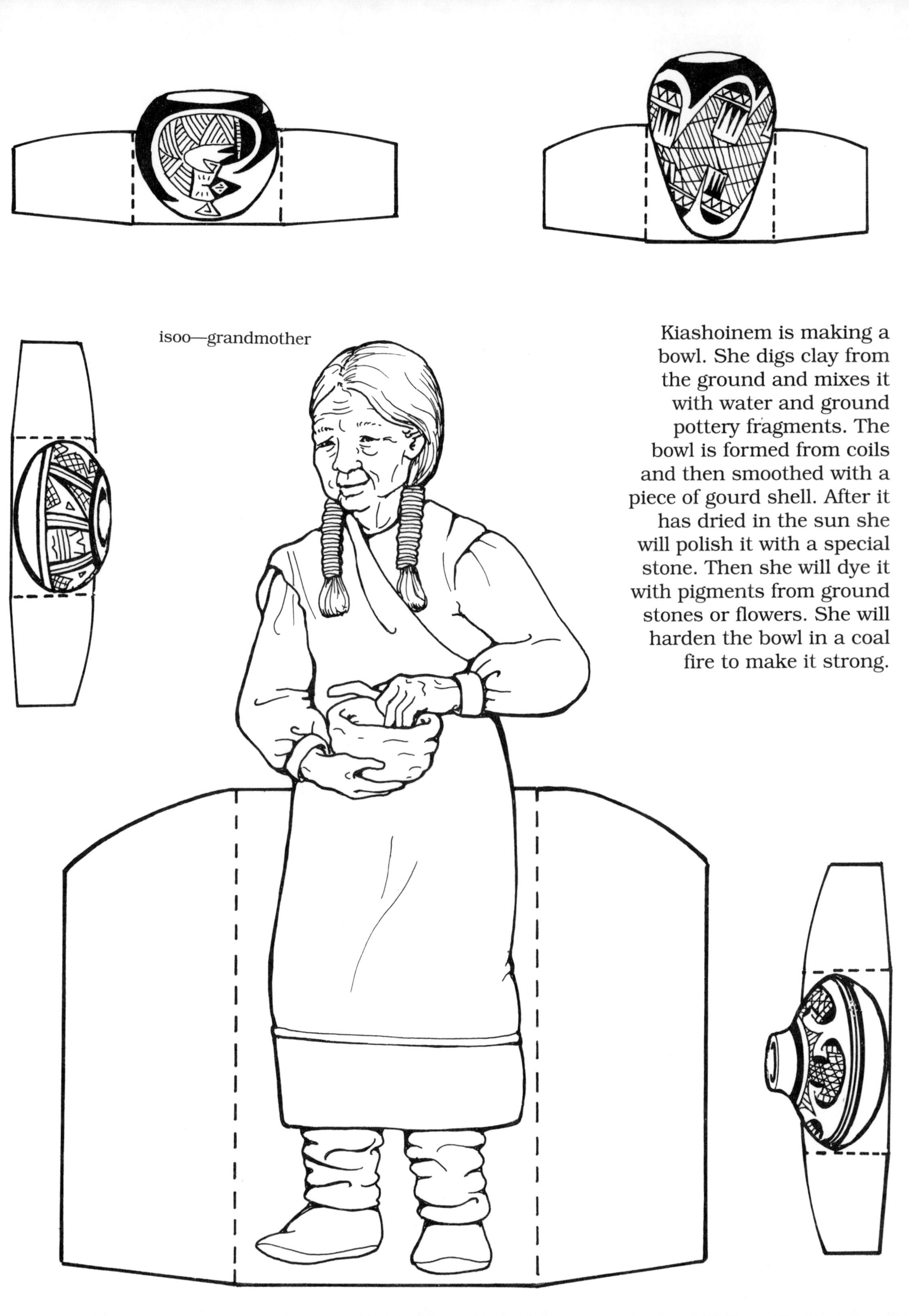

Kiashoinem is making a bowl. She digs clay from the ground and mixes it with water and ground pottery fragments. The bowl is formed from coils and then smoothed with a piece of gourd shell. After it has dried in the sun she will polish it with a special stone. Then she will dye it with pigments from ground stones or flowers. She will harden the bowl in a coal fire to make it strong.

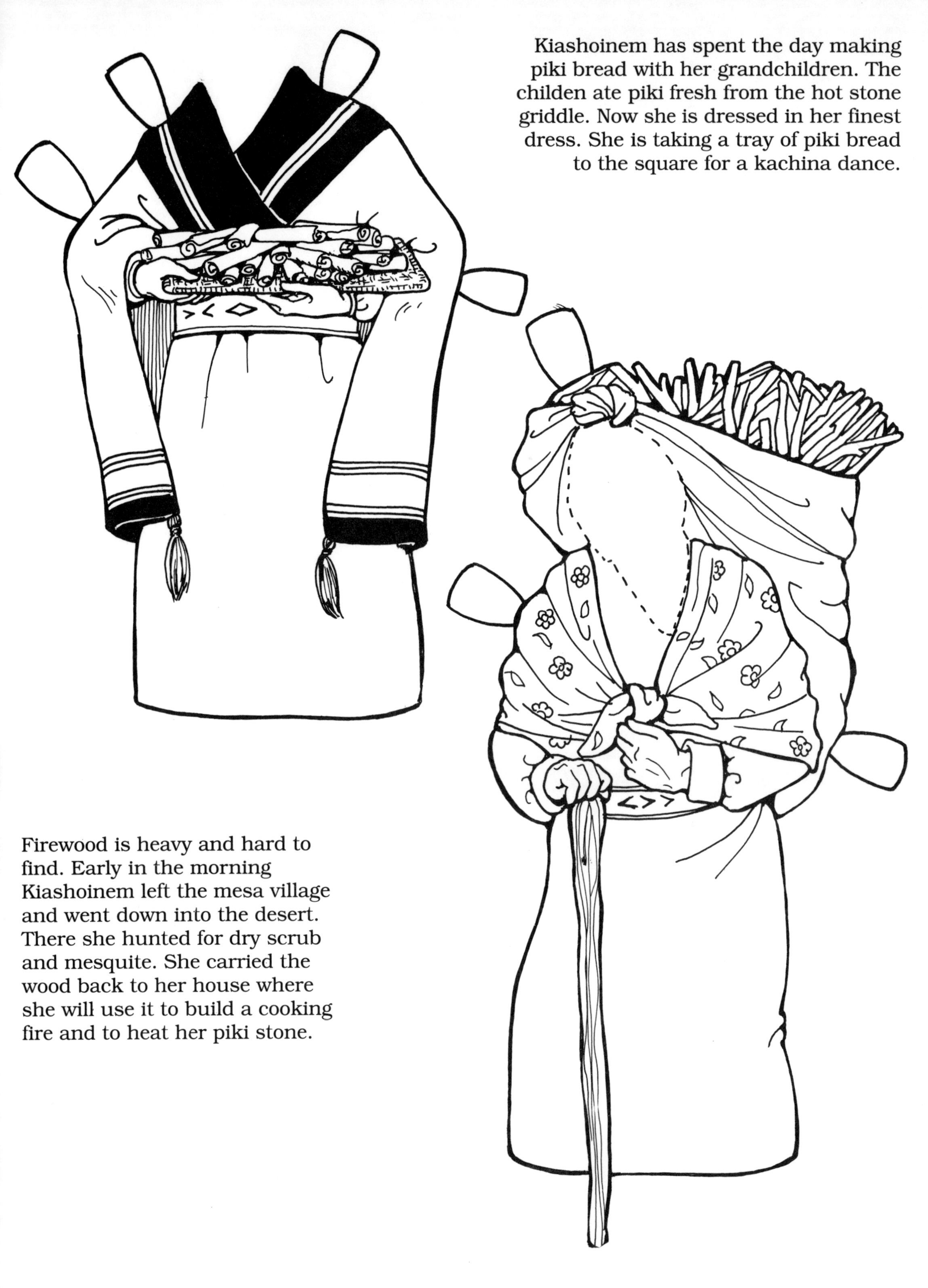

Kiashoinem has spent the day making piki bread with her grandchildren. The childen ate piki fresh from the hot stone griddle. Now she is dressed in her finest dress. She is taking a tray of piki bread to the square for a kachina dance.

Firewood is heavy and hard to find. Early in the morning Kiashoinem left the mesa village and went down into the desert. There she hunted for dry scrub and mesquite. She carried the wood back to her house where she will use it to build a cooking fire and to heat her piki stone.

In the village plaza Choro and other women dance the Lakon basket dance. Each woman is dressed in her most beautiful dress and jewelry. Everyone carries a special tray of woven sumac and rabbitbrush. The women sing and dance holding the trays in front of their faces. At the end of the dance presents are given to the men of the village.

Choro has a basket of peaches to share with her children. Kachi and Honmana will help their mother cut the pits from the rest of the peaches.

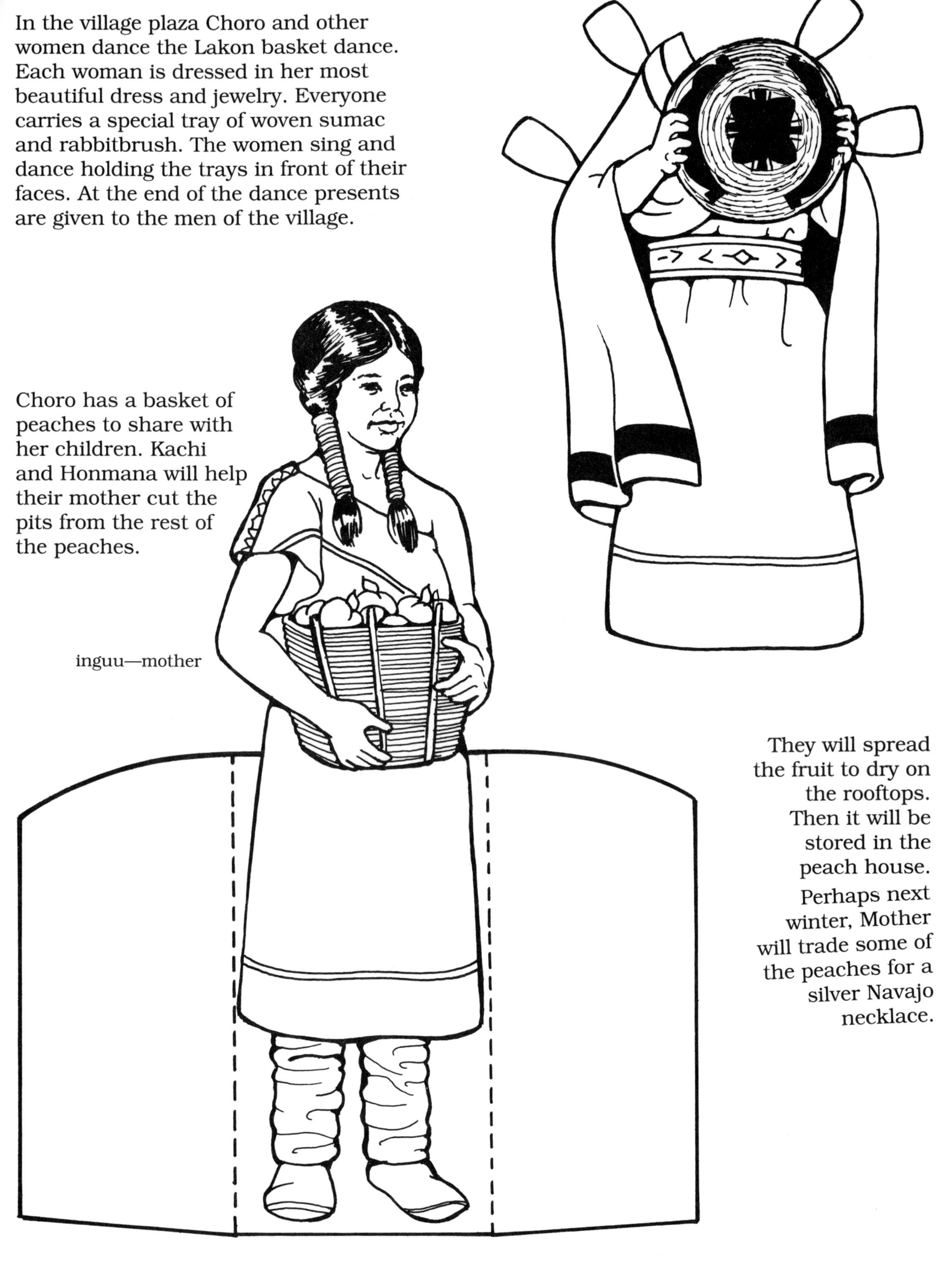

inguu—mother

They will spread the fruit to dry on the rooftops. Then it will be stored in the peach house. Perhaps next winter, Mother will trade some of the peaches for a silver Navajo necklace.

Kachi's father, Tuqui, is going to farm. He holds seeds and a digging stick called a sooya. Tuqui will plant squash, chiles, sunflowers, beans and corn. Hopi corn comes in a rainbow of colors—red, yellow, rose, white, blue, black and mottled.

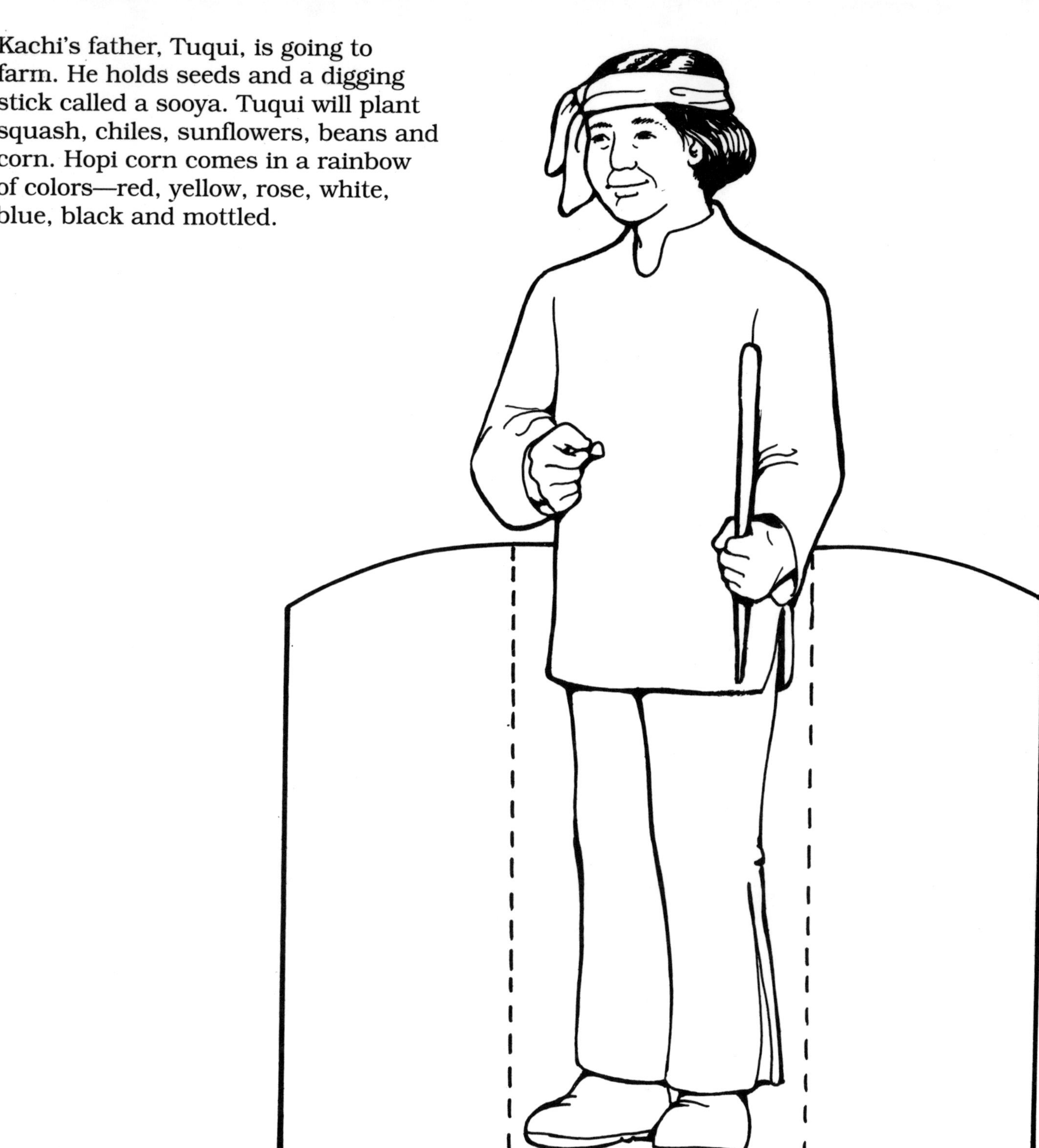

inaa—father

Taqui is carving a kachina doll to give to one of his female relatives. He carves the doll from a cottonwood root. Then he smoothes it with a rasp and paints it with paints he makes from plants and stones. Later he will decorate the doll with feathers. A special flat doll with no feathers is given to babies. This is called a cradle doll.

Tuqui is getting ready to spin yarn from wool. The wool is sheared from the sheep. Then it is cleaned and combed. When Tuqui is done spinning he will dye the yarn with boiled plants. After the yarn is dry he will take it down into the kiva. There he will weave cloth to make clothes for his entire family.

Honapsi has traded some corn to get a fine piece of leather from a Navajo. He cut the leather to make himself a pair of moccasins. The bottom of the moccasin is tough rawhide to protect his feet. The rest of the leather is soft.

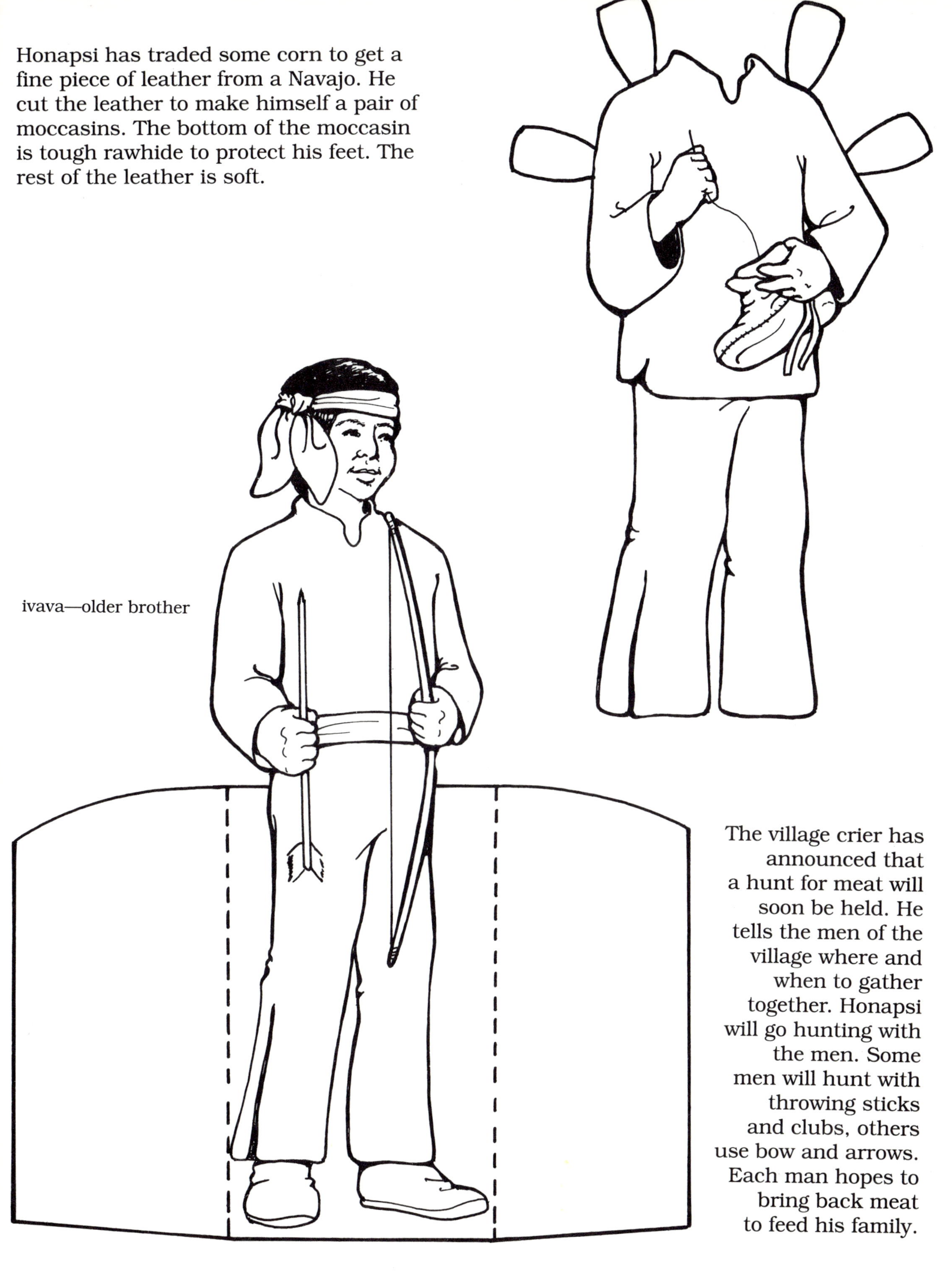

ivava—older brother

The village crier has announced that a hunt for meat will soon be held. He tells the men of the village where and when to gather together. Honapsi will go hunting with the men. Some men will hunt with throwing sticks and clubs, others use bow and arrows. Each man hopes to bring back meat to feed his family.

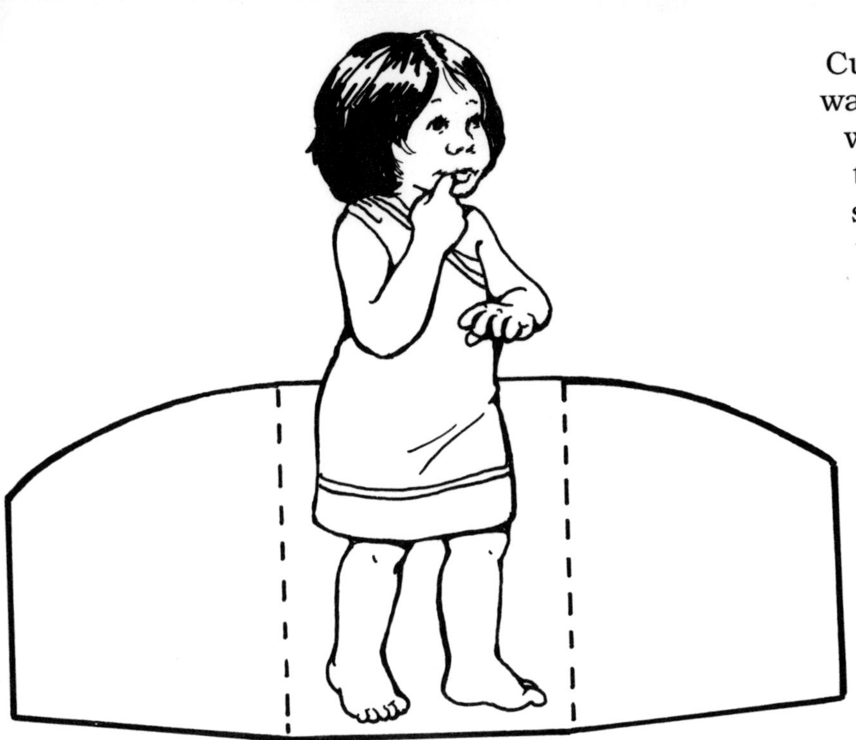

Cuya loves to walk to the well and get water with her sisters. While the older women line up and take turns filling their water jugs, Cuya splashes and sings to herself. When Kachi goes to the family cistern to fetch rainwater Cuya wants to come along.

itupko—younger brother
younger sister

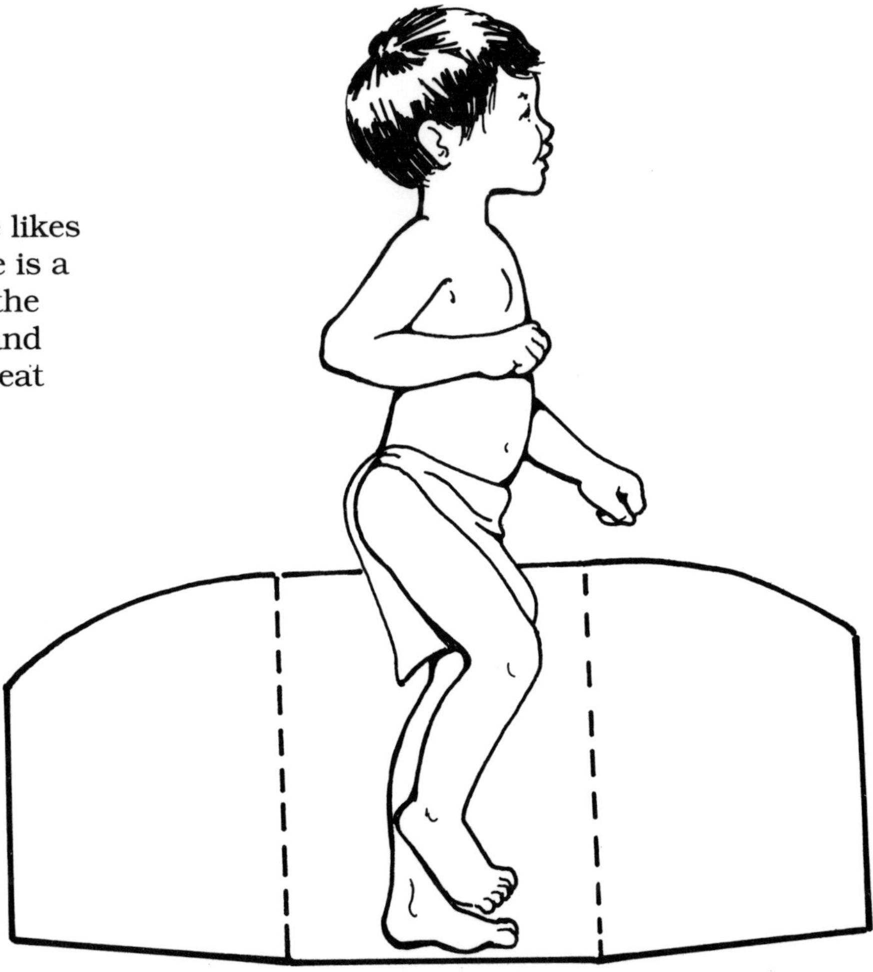

Honhoya plays most of the day. Sometimes he makes mischief. He likes to run and be very noisy. When he is a little older father will take him to the fields. There he can run and yell and chase away birds or animals that eat the plants.

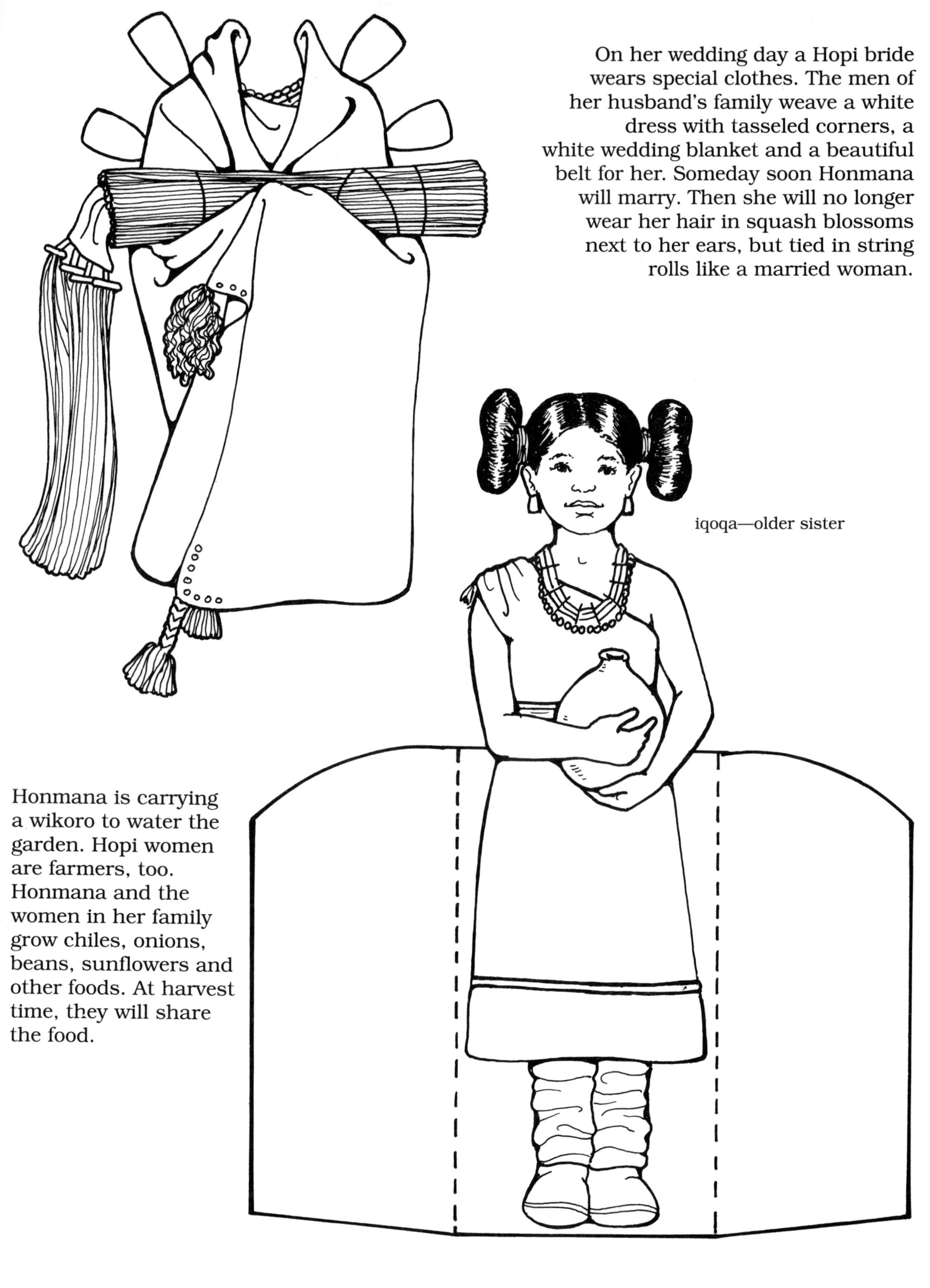

On her wedding day a Hopi bride wears special clothes. The men of her husband's family weave a white dress with tasseled corners, a white wedding blanket and a beautiful belt for her. Someday soon Honmana will marry. Then she will no longer wear her hair in squash blossoms next to her ears, but tied in string rolls like a married woman.

iqoqa—older sister

Honmana is carrying a wikoro to water the garden. Hopi women are farmers, too. Honmana and the women in her family grow chiles, onions, beans, sunflowers and other foods. At harvest time, they will share the food.

In the middle of summer the Niman ceremony is held and the kachinas return to sleep on their mountain for the rest of the year. The older boys and men dress and paint themselves like kachinas, and they dance the kachina dances. Each year they dance the cycle of dances from Soyal to Niman.

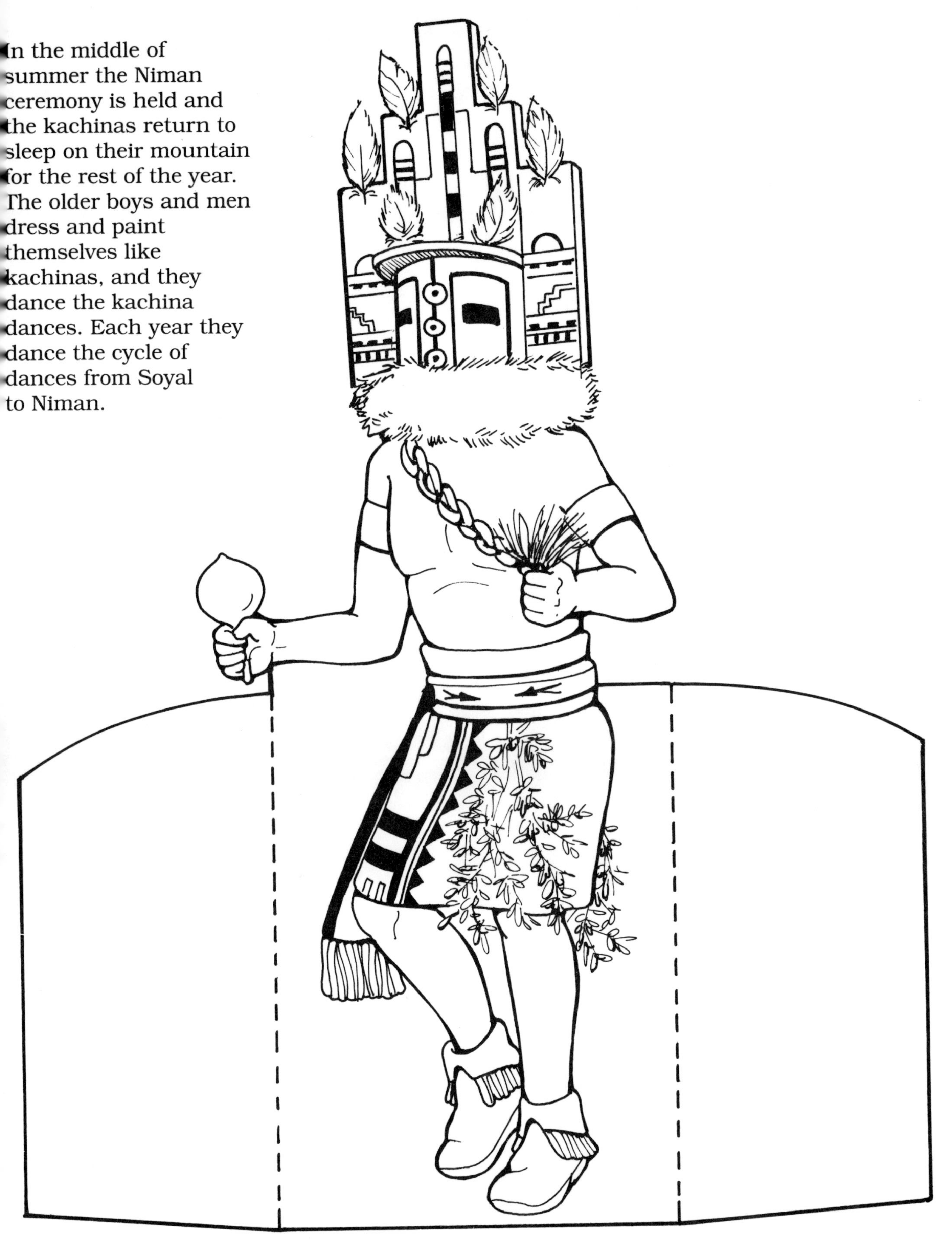

Each kachina doll has a name, and each name has a meaning. Some kachinas represent heroic characters or forces of nature.

Kwahu—Eagle Kachina

There is a sun kachina, a cloud kachina, a butterfly kachina and many more. There is even a mudhead clown kachina.

Soyal—Solstice or Returning Kachina

Tawa—Sun Kachina

Kachinas are supernatural beings that are very important to the Hopi.

These kachina dolls are not drawn to scale for Kachi. They are miniature dolls for you to color and cut. Today's kachina dolls are modern representations of an ancient and evolving art.

These are some of the crops that Kachi's family grow for food.

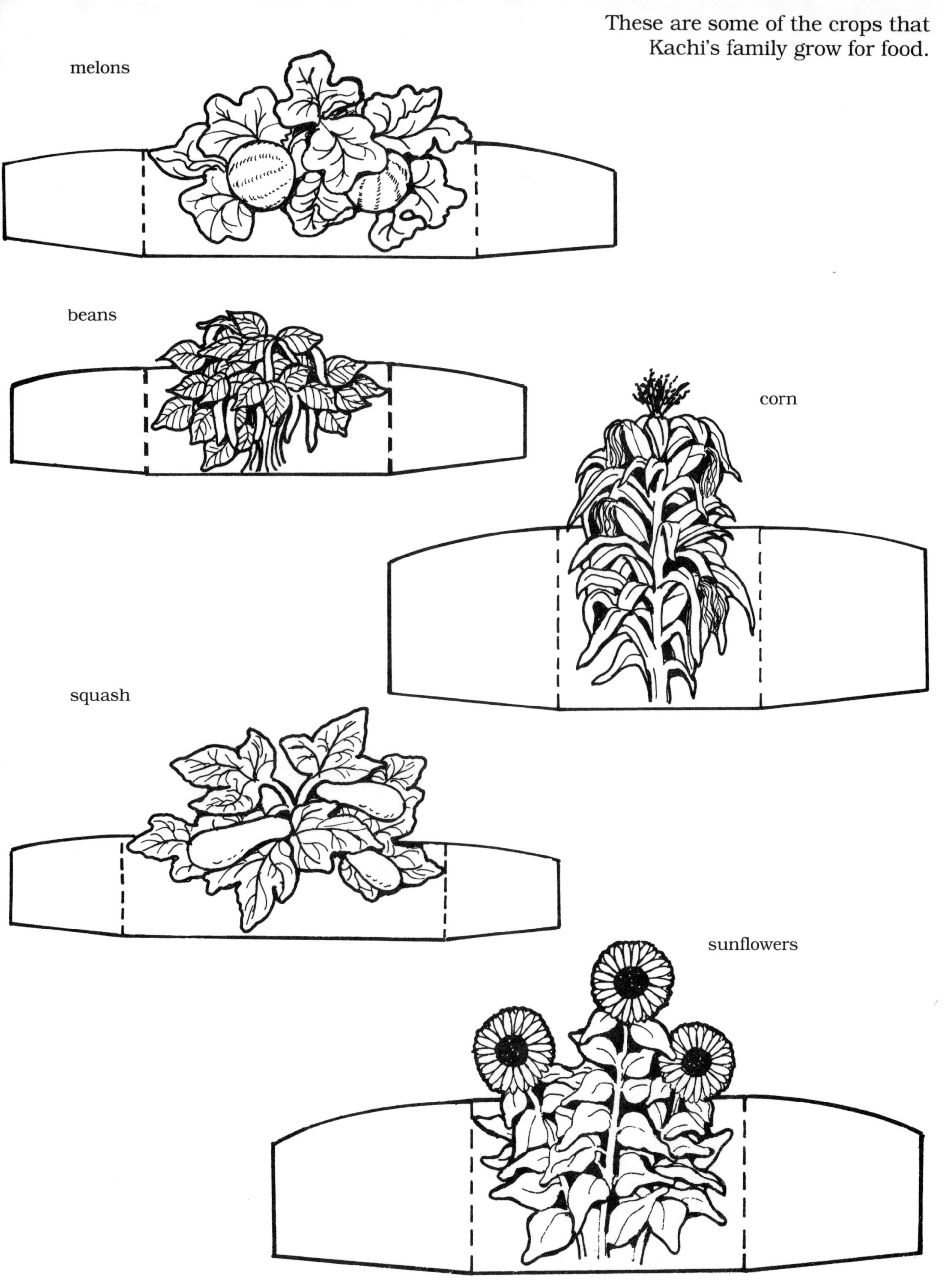

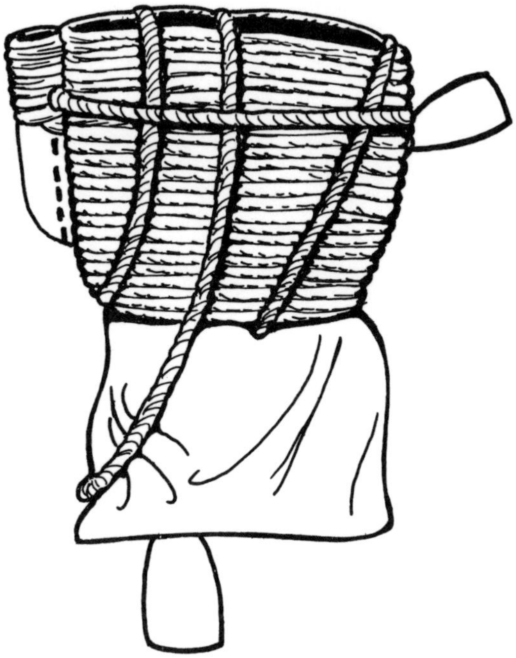

The burro is very stubborn. Honhoya jumps on him and pretends he is a horse, but the burro won't move. When it is time to work the burro walks very slowly to the fields. But he runs all the way home when it is time to eat dinner.